THE ULTIMATE BEGII   'S®

BARRE CHORD BASICS

BY AARON STANG

Additional text and editorial by Louis Martinez
Project Manager: Aaron Stang
Technical Editor: Jack Allen
Engraver: Musical Arts Consultants

Contents

Foreword

In this book you are going to learn how to use "moveable" barre chords. "Moveable" chord forms are especial-ly useful because after learning just a few simple fingerings, you can then move those fingerings around the neck, creating virtually every chord you'll ever need. Each new chord is taught in the context of common chord progressions that every guitarist should know. With the basic knowledge you'll acquire here, you'll soon be able to play any song in any key. Chords are a critical element of playing the guitar, and the more chords you "have under your fingers," the more fun you'll have with your guitar.

Chapter 1
Root Six Barre Chords

Major Barre Chord:

What's so nice about moveable barre chords is that you don't have to learn that many of them. Since there are no open strings, by learning a few fingerings you can move them up and down the neck of the guitar. All you have to do is place them by their root name. The root is usually the lowest note of the chord. Below is an example of a G barre chord:

The root of this chord is under your first finger on the sixth string. If you move this chord up a half step to the fourth fret, it becomes G♯ (or A♭). Moving up in half steps from G♯ you have: A, B♭, B, C, and so on. Everytime you move the barre chord up or down the neck, the root name changes. By learning one fingering you can play all twelve major chords.

"E" Type Barre Chord:

The barre chord we just learned is derived from the basic E major chord.
The root is on the sixth string:

E Chord Refingered:

Now, take this chord and switch your fingers around. Instead of using your first, second, and third fingers as indicated previously, use your second, third, and fourth fingers as shown below. This is the same chord but it leaves your first finger free:

Root Six Barre Chord:

Maintain the second fingering of the E major chord and slide your hand up one fret. Since your first finger is free, lay it across the first fret. You now have an F major chord. The root of this chord is on the sixth string under your first finger. You'll find this F chord difficult to play at first but, as you slide this fingering up the neck, it becomes easier. In time you will be able to play these chords proficiently:

Tip: When playing barre chords, lay your first finger just behind the fret, not on top of it, or too far away from the fret. Also, try not to lay your index finger flat on the neck. Turn your finger slightly to the side where the hard part of the finger is. Pinch hard between your index finger and thumb.

Notes on the Sixth String:

It is important to know the notes on the sixth string. The "root six" barre chords are named by these notes. In the illustration below you will see the notes on the sixth string. Practice the root six barre chord through all twelve frets and be able to name each chord by its correct root name.

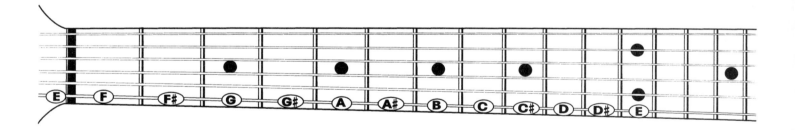

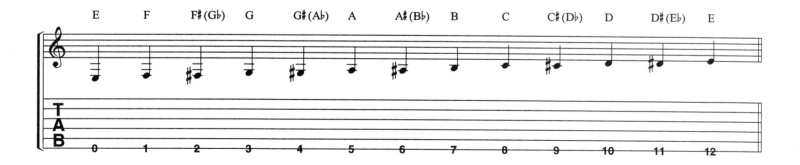

Chord Progression Using Major Barre Chords:

Here's a chord progression using the root six major barre chord you've learned. This progression is very similar to a song by Otis Redding called "Sittin' On The Dock Of The Bay."

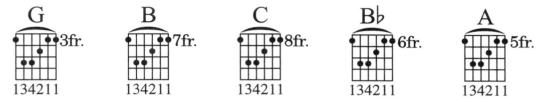

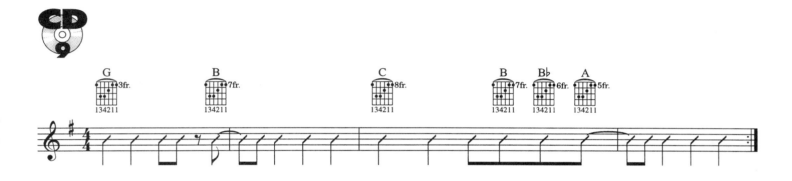

Root Six Minor Barre Chord:

To play a minor barre chord, all you have to do is lift your second finger off the root six barre chord. For example, take the G major barre chord you learned earlier and lift your second finger off. Now you have a G minor chord. This is still a root six barre chord, and can be slid up and down the neck:

Chord Progression Using Major and Minor Barre Chords:

Now we're going to use G, Am, and Bm in a chord progression. Remember, once you know your chord forms they can be moved up and down the neck.

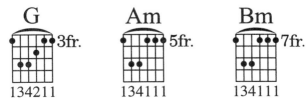

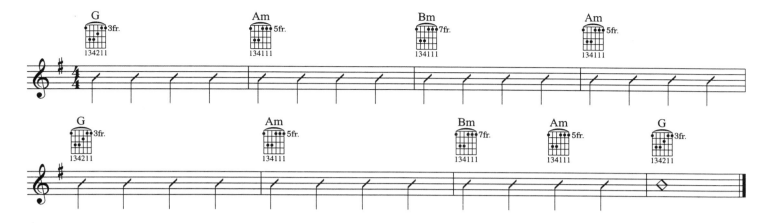

Tip: Playing chords by themselves is not that difficult. The hard part is changing from one chord to another. Practicing this progression will help you to develop the facility needed to change chords smoothly.

Root Six Dominant 7th Barre Chord:

Play the G major barre chord and lift off your fourth finger. Strum through the six strings and you have a G7 chord. Press your first finger down firmly so that the sixth, fourth, second, and first strings ring out.

Chord Progression Using Dominant 7th Barre Chord:

This is a classic rock & roll progression making use of major, minor, and dominant 7th barre chords. The chords are C, Am, F, and G7. These are the three root six chord forms you've learned up to this point.

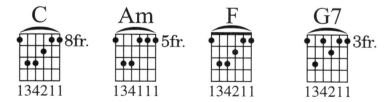

Chapter 2
Root Five Barre Chords

Root Five Major Barre Chord:

In the last chapter you learned barre chords with roots on the sixth string. In this chapter we're going to look at barre chords with roots on the fifth string. Here's a C major barre chord:

The root of this chord is under your first finger on the fifth string. If you move this chord up a half step to the fourth fret, it becomes C♯ (or D♭). Continuing moving up in half steps from C♯ you have D, E♭, E, and so on. Everytime you move the barre chord up or down the neck the root name changes. By learning this fingering you can play all twelve pitches.

"A" Type Barre Chord:

The chord you learned above is derived from the A major chord. The root is on the fifth string:

Root Five Barre Chord:

Play the A major chord and slide your hand up one fret. Take your first finger and lay it across the first fret. You now have a B♭ major chord. Move up a half step and you have a B major chord and another half step a C major chord. The root of this chord is on the fifth string under your first finger. Practice this chord and in time you will be able to play it more proficiently:

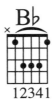

Alternate Fingering:

Another popular way to finger this chord is to use two barres together. The first finger barres across five strings while the third finger lays across the fourth, third, and second strings two frets higher. Arch your third finger slightly so the first string rings out. If the note on the first string is not heard, don't worry. As time goes on, your fingers will become more limber.

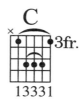

Notes on the Fifth String:

It is just as important to know the notes on the fifth string as it is with the sixth. In the illustration below you will see the notes on the fifth string. Practice the root five barre chord through all twelve frets and be able to name each chord by its correct root name.

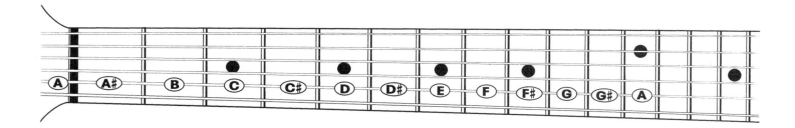

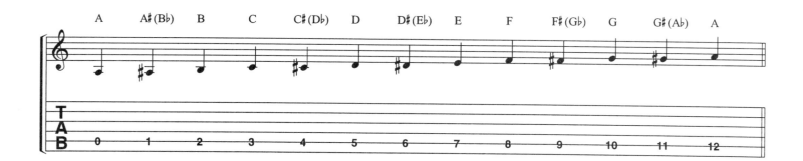

Chord Progression Using Major Barre Chords:

Here's the same chord progression we used in Chapter One which is similar to Otis Redding's song called "Sittin' On The Dock Of The Bay."

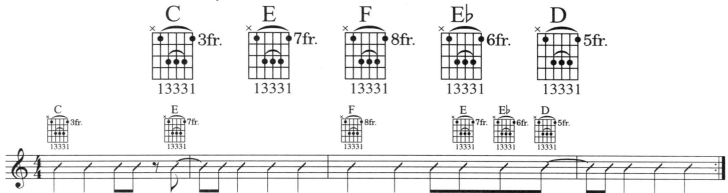

Root Five Minor Barre Chord:

To play a root five minor barre chord, first finger the C major chord you have learned. Now move the note on the second string down a half step to the fourth fret. To do this you need to lift off your third finger barre and place your second finger on the fourth fret, second string. Add your third and fourth finger on the fourth and third strings' fifth fret. Make sure you press firmly. Since this is a root five barre chord, the sixth string is not played.

Cm
3fr.
13421

Chord Progression Using Major and Minor Barre Chords:

This is the same diatonic progression we used earlier but with C, Dm, and Em . Remember, once you know your chord forms, they can be moved up and down the neck.

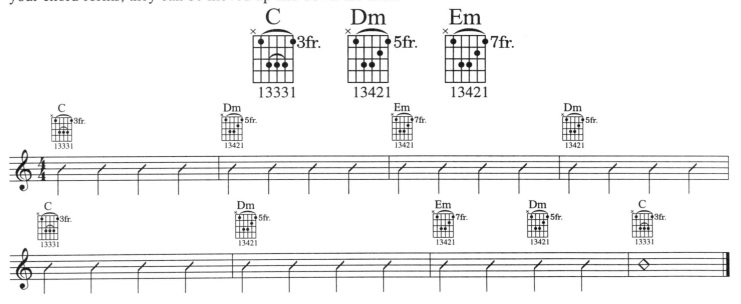

Root Five Dominant 7th Barre Chord:

Take the C major barre chord and lift your third finger barre, leaving the tip of the finger down on the fourth string, fifth fret. Add your fourth finger on the second string, fifth fret while the first finger barres five strings on the third fret. Strum through the five strings and you have a C7 chord. Press your first finger down firmly so the fifth, third, and first strings ring out:

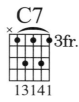

Chord Progression Using Dominant 7th Barre Chord:

Here's a chord progression making use of root five major, minor, and dominant 7th barre chords:

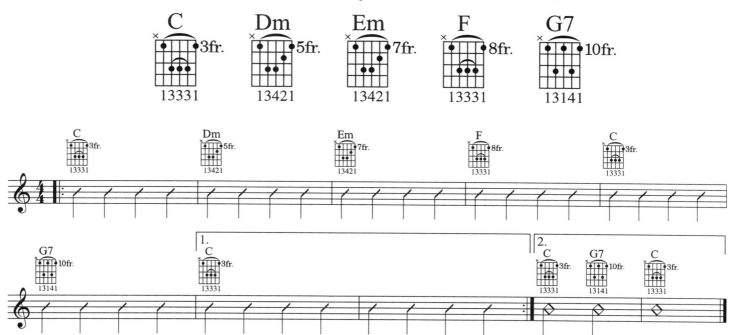

Chord Progression Combining Root Five and Root Six:

To play the last progression with root five chords, you have to move your hand up and down a lot, especially between C and G7. Well, there are easier ways of playing this same progression by minimizing the amount of movement. Since you already know the root five and the root six barre chords, you can mix them together. All you have to do is find the closest position to where your hand is. Play the last progression again, mixing the two forms together. So for C, Dm, Em, and F you can use the root five barre chords and for G7 use the root six barre chord. This will make the jump between C and G7 easier.

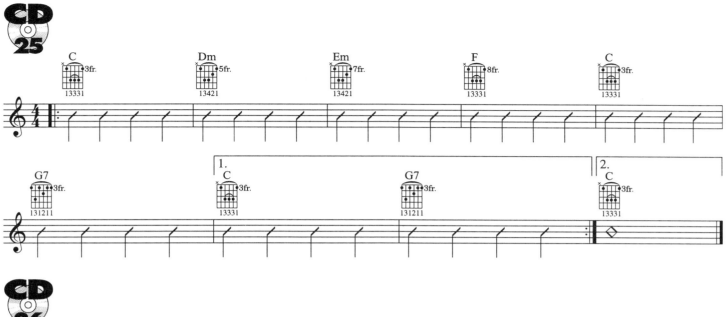

C, Am, F, and G7 Chord Progression:

Here's the classic rock & roll progression you played earlier but this time you're going to mix the root five and root six barre chords. For C, use the root five barre chord. A minor can be played with the root five form but it means jumping up to the twelfth fret. To minimize movement, play A minor using the root six barre chord on the fifth fret. Also, use root six barre chords for F (1st fret) and G7 (3rd fret).

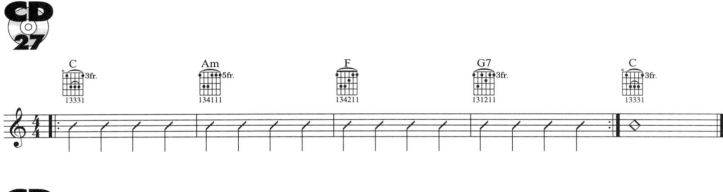

G, Am, Bm, C, and D7 Chord Progression:

This is another common chord progression in the key of G to help you get a better understanding of the root five and six barre chord forms.

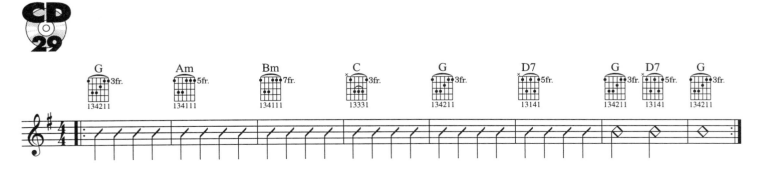

At this point you can virtually play any song, in any key, knowing a total of only six fingerings. Since they can be played from any root, you can multiply that by twelve and you now know a total of seventy-two chords.

Chapter 3
Power Chords

What Is a Power Chord?:

Power chords and boogie progressions have been the key to electric guitar since Chuck Berry invented rock & roll back in the fifties. These chords usually consist of two or three notes with emphasis on the bass strings of the guitar. These are two-note chords (root and 5th) and are indicated with a "5". For example, E5 consists of the root E and the fifth which is B. Typically, when playing these types of chords, you want to mute the strings. It gives the chord a little more clarity and definition. To mute the strings, place the palm of your picking hand lightly on the strings by the bridge of the guitar:

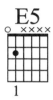

Movable Power Chords:

Let's take this E5 chord and move it to G5. Take the root (E) which is the sixth string open and move it up three frets to G. Now place your first finger on it. The 5th is always two frets up on the next string so place your third finger on the fifth fret, fifth string. This is a G5 chord and it can be moved up and down the neck. For example, if you move the G5 up two frets up you have an A5 chord:

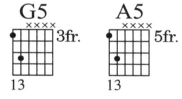

E5, G5, and A5 Chord Progression:

Here's a popular chord progression used in rock and blues. It originated with John Lee Hooker and lots of artists used it; like ZZ Top and Stevie Ray Vaughn, to name a few. It consists of three chords: E5, G5, and A5.

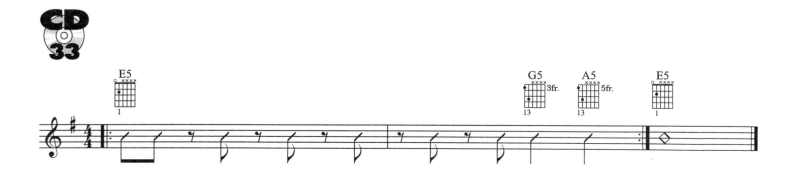

Tip: When playing power chords, try using a little distortion and notice how powerful they sound. Use some palm muting and these chords will come to life.

A5, C5, and D5 Root Five Power Chords:

The A5 chord is very similar to the E5 chord. The only difference is that the root is on the fifth string. Let's do the same thing we did with the E5 chord. Take the A5 chord and move up two frets where the root is on the third fret, fifth string and you have a C5 chord. Move the C5 chord up two more frets and you have a D5 chord.

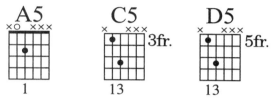

A5, C5, and D5 Chord Progression:

This is the same progression we used previously in E but now in the key of A:

Mixing the E5 and A5 Chord Progression:

Here's a chord progression using these two patterns:

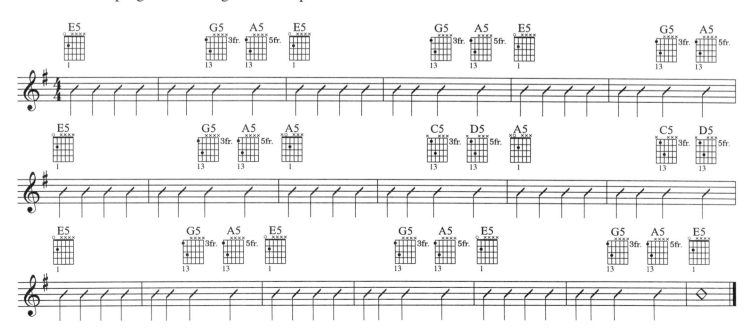

Rock & Roll Boogie:

While playing G5, extend your fourth finger out two frets on the fifth string. The chord then becomes G6. Now, alternate back and forth between G5 and G6. You need to keep your first finger planted on the root of the chord and the third finger on the fifth of the chord.

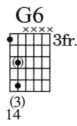

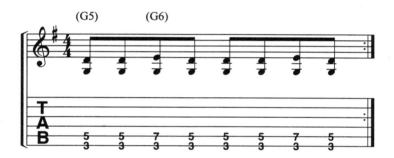

Alternate G6 Fingering:

If you have problems making the stretch with your third and fourth finger. You can use your second finger in place of your third.

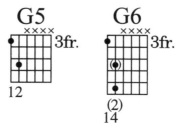

G7 Power Chord:

If you feel comfortable with the alternate G6 fingering, you can try stretching your fourth finger out one more fret to the eighth fret.

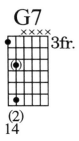

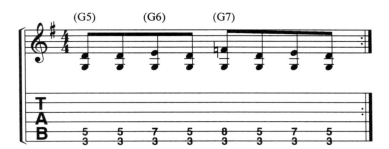

C5 and C6 Power Chords:

Like we did with the G5 and G6, the same can be done with C5 and C6 chords. They use the same fingering as G5 and G6 but the root is on the fifth string. Practice alternating between C5 and C6.

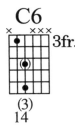

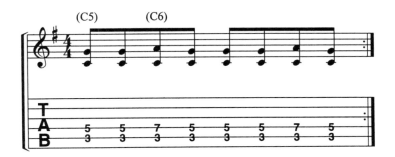

Alternate C6 Fingering:

If you have problems making the stretch with your third and fourth finger. You can use your second finger in place of your third.

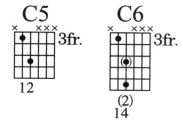

C7 Power Chord:

If you feel comfortable with the alternate C6 fingering, you can try stretching your fourth finger out one more fret to the eighth fret.

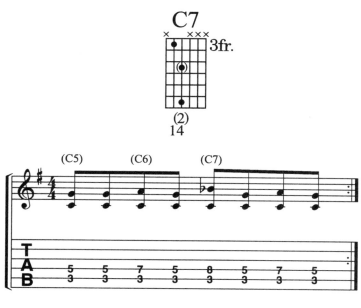

Classic Boogie Progression:

This progression contains only three chords: G5, C5, and D5. It is usually twelve measures in length. There are thousands of songs that use this boogie progression. D5 is two frets up from C5 on the fifth string. Play this progression with the patterns you've learned.

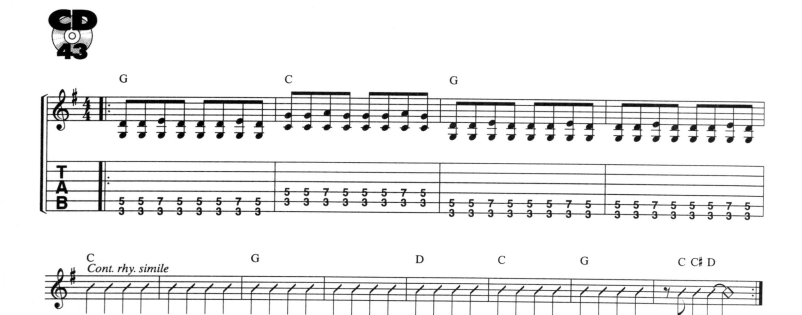

Chapter 4
Jazz Chords

Up to this point you have learned barre chords and power chords. In this chapter I'm going to introduce a few new chord voicings. They will come in handy when you want a jazzier sound, whether it be a blues or a jazz standard.

A13 Chord:

Play the A7 barre chord you learned earlier. While holding the chord add your fourth finger to the second string two frets higher than the barre. That is the note that makes this a 13th chord. This is a popular and very pretty sounding chord. This is a root six type chord and it is movable:

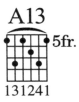

D9 Chord:

This is also a movable chord. The root is on the fifth string. Play the D7 chord and notice where the root is. Lift your fingers off and place your second finger on the root (D). Place your first finger on the fourth string, fourth fret. Now take your third finger and barre the first three strings on the fifth fret:

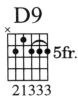

Root Six Minor 7 Chord:

You have already learned a root six minor chord. This chord is basically the same fingering but without your fourth finger. Remember, the root is on the sixth string. Below is a Bm7, which is on the seventh fret. Squeeze hard between the thumb and index finger.

Chord Progression Using "Jazz" Chords:

This progression combines almost all the barre chords you have learned. This is a common progression but a little more sophisticated. A classic use of this progression is "Stormy Monday Blues" originally written by T-Bone Walker. Check out the great version of this song is by the Allman Brothers on "Live at the Fillmore." It can be played a variety of ways but this is the basic chord progression.

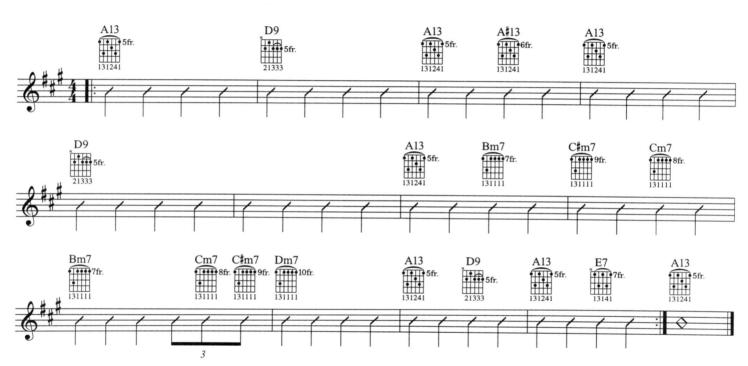

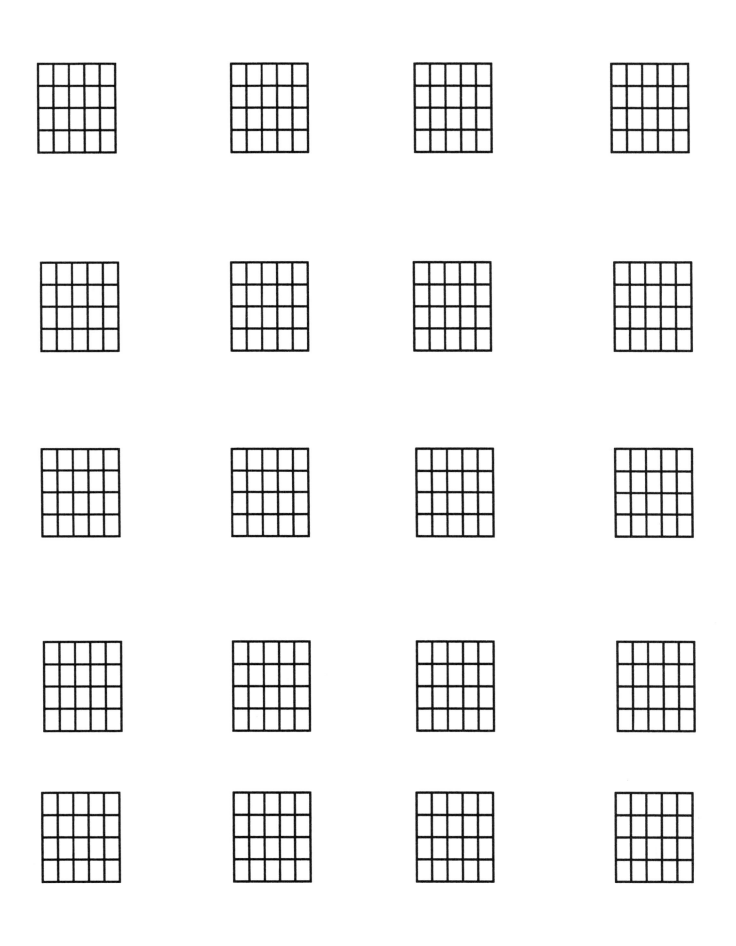

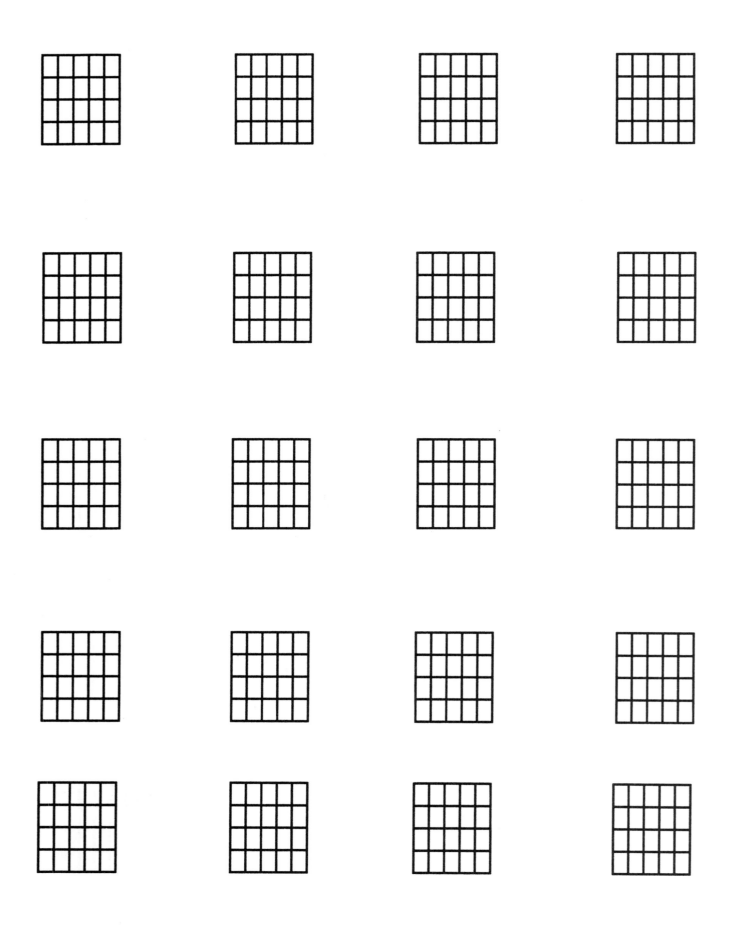

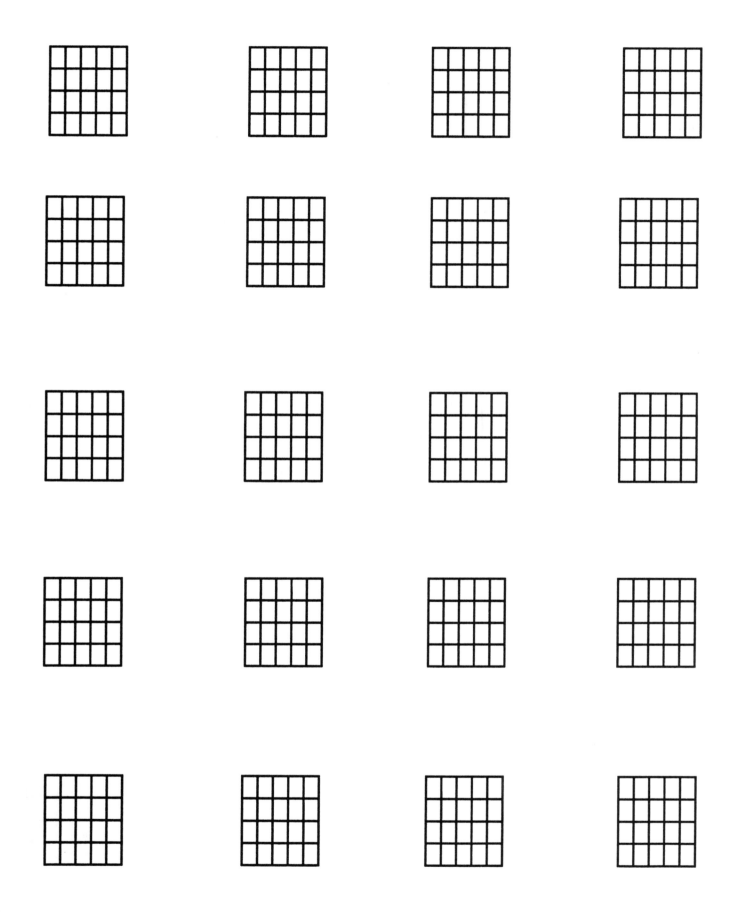

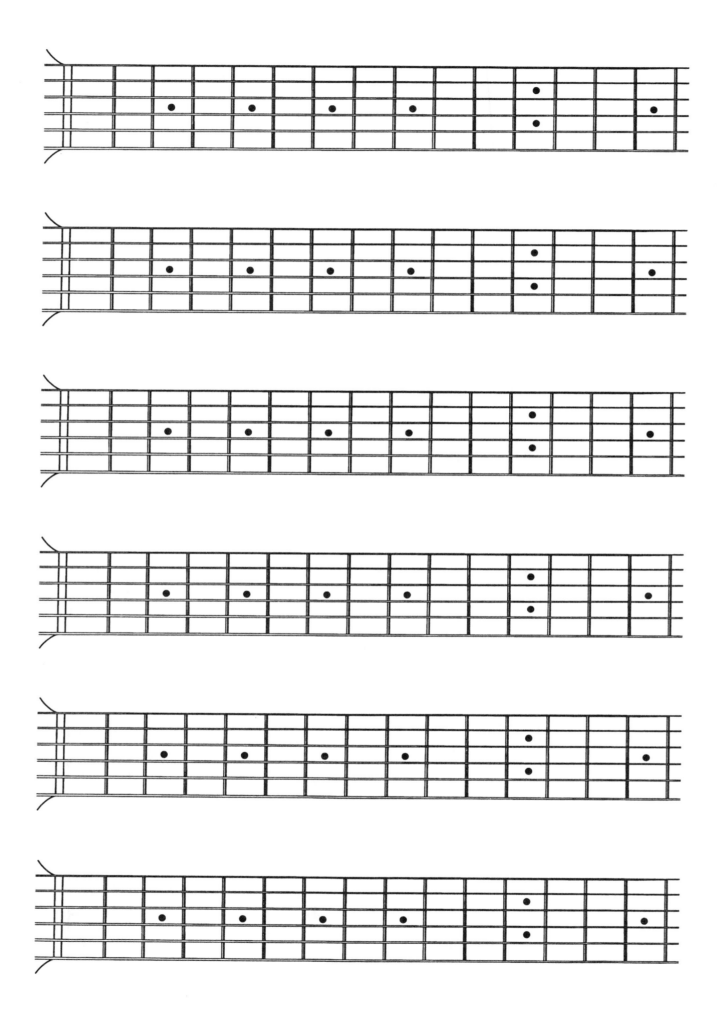

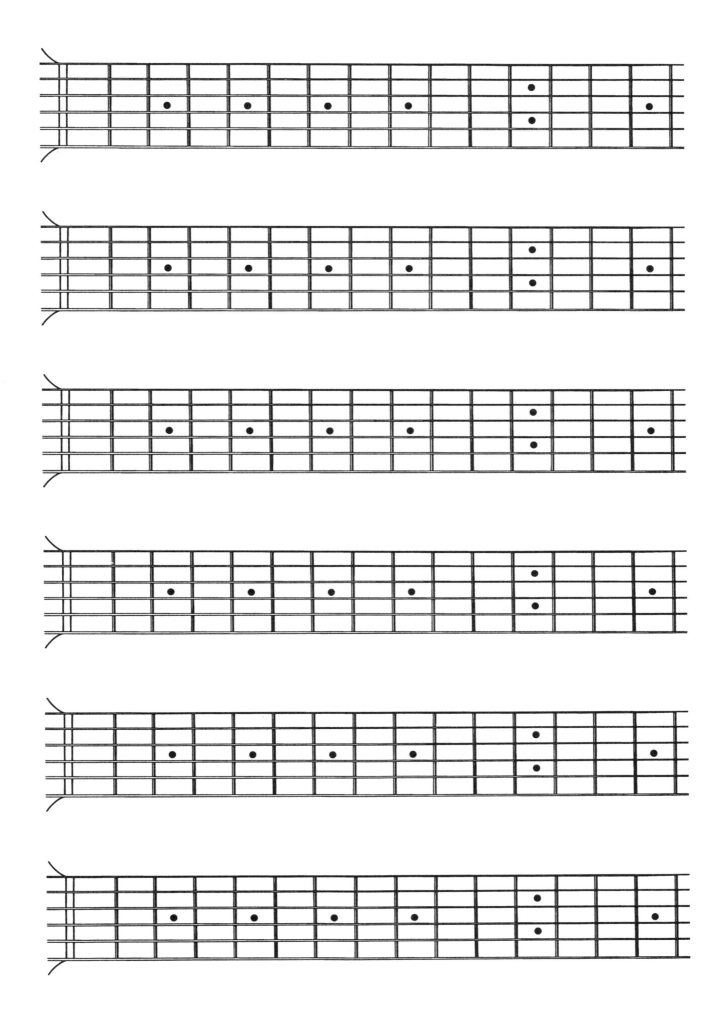

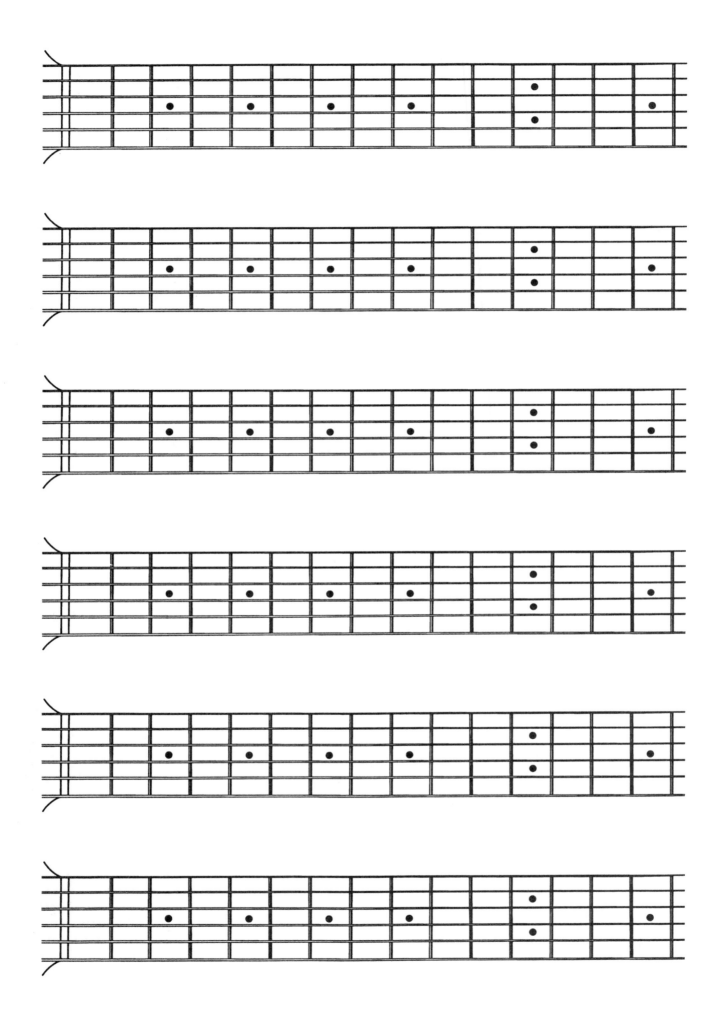

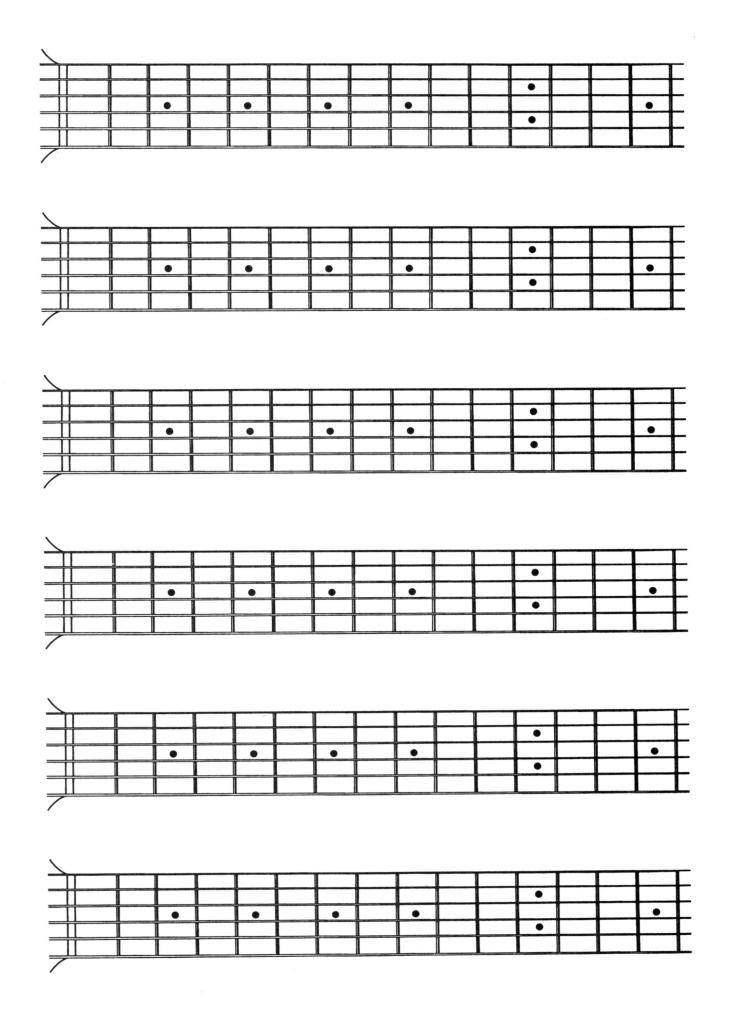

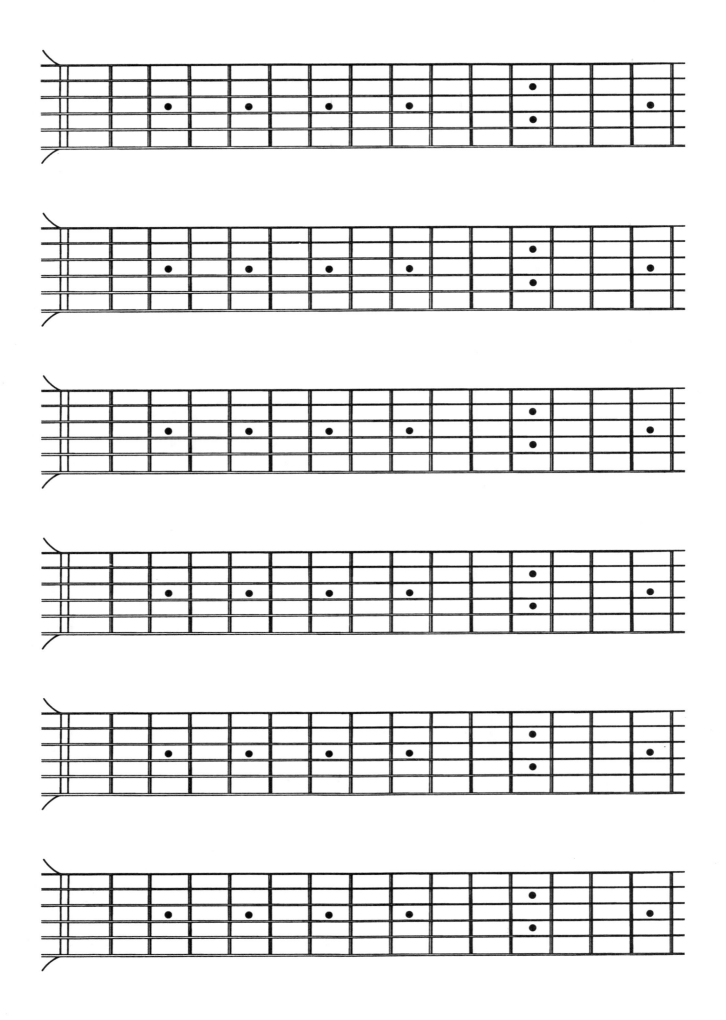